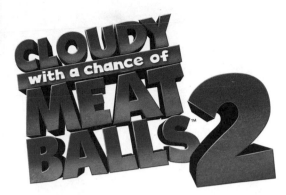

Flint Lockwood
Saves the World . . . AGAIN!

adapted by Maggie Testa
illustrated by Aaron Spurgeon

Simon Spotlight
New York   London   Toronto   Sydney   New Delhi

Read the original book by
Judi Barrett and Ron Barrett.

SIMON SPOTLIGHT
An imprint of Simon & Schuster Children's Publishing Division
1230 Avenue of the Americas, New York, New York 10020
TM & © 2013 Sony Pictures Animation Inc. All Rights Reserved.
All rights reserved, including the right of reproduction in whole or in part in any form.
SIMON SPOTLIGHT and colophon are registered trademarks of Simon & Schuster, Inc.
For information about special discounts for bulk purchases, please contact Simon & Schuster Special Sales at 1-866-506-1949 or
business@simonandschuster.com.
Manufactured in The United States 0713 LAK
First Edition
2 4 6 8 10 9 7 5 3 1
ISBN 978-1-4424-9548-7
ISBN 978-1-4424-9647-7 (eBook)

Flint Lockwood made an invention that turned water into food. It was called the FLDSMDFR (the Flint Lockwood Diatonic Super Mutating Dynamic Food Replicator). Unfortunately, he had to destroy it when gigantic food started raining down. But he made something even better in the process . . . friends!

Flint and his new friends were planning their future when a helicopter landed in the middle of the mess. Out stepped Chester V, Flint's idol and the head of Live Corp!

"I've brought my Thinkquanauts to Swallow Falls to help clean up the leftovers!" Chester explained. "You will all be temporarily relocated to sunny San Franjose."

Chester wanted Flint to come work for him,
telling him that he could become an orange-vested
Thinkquanaut if he worked hard!
"This is the best day ever!" exclaimed Flint.

For the next six months, Flint toiled day and night in his little cubicle, working on inventions that could change the world. He even invented a Celebrationator, a party in a box for any occasion.

Then it was time for the Thinkquanaut ceremony. Flint was sure that Chester would make him a Thinkquanaut, but Chester chose someone else.

Flint was devastated. "No reason to celebrate," he told Steve, his lab partner.

When Steve heard the word "celebrate" he pressed the button on the Celebrationator, covering Flint in glitter.

Later that night, Chester's second-in-command, Barb, brought Flint to Chester's office. Chester showed Flint a video of a cheespider attacking Chester's clean-up crew in Swallow Falls.

"Living food?" asked Flint. "This could only mean one thing . . . the FLDSMDFR is still operating!"

Chester explained that the living food was trying to learn to swim. They had to stop it before the food made it to the mainland and began destroying everything.

"My Thinkquanauts have invented a stop button," said Chester. "Whoever finds the FLDSMDFR and plugs in the stop button will become a Thinkquanaut!"

"I'll do it!" volunteered Flint.

Soon, Flint and his friends were back at Swallow Falls. Where there once had been a town, there was now a dense jungle. Giant pieces of food decorated the landscape. The gang was headed to Flint's lab when they discovered a living baby strawberry. Sam named it Barry, before realizing that it had stolen Chester's stop button.

The gang chased Barry to a watering hole filled with living food. There were wildebeets, flamangos, watermelophants, bananostritches, and hippotatomuses enjoying the water. In the sky above, shrimpanzees leaped from tree to tree.

"Wow, I can't believe the FLDSMDFR created all of this," observed Flint.

But there was something else that had caught up to them . . . the menacing cheespider! The gang ran away, right into a dead end.

Just when they thought they were toast, a helicopter descended from the sky. The cheespider retreated into the jungle.

"Chester V!" cried Flint happily. "You're here!"

"By the looks of things, just in time," replied Chester.

Flint nodded. Now that they had Chester's stop button back from Barry, it was time to get to his lab and locate the FLDSMDFR.

But Sam had begun to wonder if they really should shut down the FLDSMDFR and destroy the food creatures. After all, Barry and most of the other creatures were friendly. It was only the cheespider that seemed upset.

The next morning, as Flint and the gang set out to find the FLDSMDFR, Sam spoke up. "What if we're making a big mistake?" she asked.

But Chester didn't want to hear that. "We are talking about food here, Ms. Sparks. Dangerous food."

Sam tried to argue with him. When Flint didn't back her up, she stormed away. So did the rest of Flint's friends.

As Sam and the gang made their way back to the boat, they heard a
roar. It was the cheespider! Everyone wanted to run, but Sam had an idea.
She walked up to the cheespider. Instead of biting her, it started to lick
her. Soon Sam was petting the friendly cheespider.

"But why did she attack us before?" asked Earl.

"Because we were dressed like them," Sam replied, pointing to the gear of the Live Corp crew in the cheespider's web.

Then Sam realized that "Live" spelled backward is "Evil!"

At that moment, Chester's crew began to zap the gang with freeze rays so they wouldn't be able to warn Flint. But there was a little berry that had seen the whole thing. . . .

Flint found the FLDSMDFR and was about to plug the stop button into the machine when he saw the living food creatures it was creating. He realized that Sam was right.

"I can't destroy an invention that is creating something so amazing," Flint told Chester.

Chester plugged the stop button into the FLDSMDFR himself. The Live Corp logo filled its screen.

Before Flint could do anything, Chester pushed him into the abyss. Luckily the living marshmallows created by the FLDSMDFR came to his rescue and brought him to safety.

Then Flint learned what had happened to his friends from Barry, and together, they hurried to Chester's new factory. While Barry freed the living food, Flint went to find his friends.

He found them tied up above Chester's food bar machine.

Flint couldn't understand why Chester needed the FLDSMDFR to make food bars.

"I can create an unlimited supply of food," explained Chester. "Then I can mass produce my greatest product yet—Food Bar Version 8.0!"

He pressed a button on the remote control, and Flint's friends began to descend toward the food bar machine.

Flint lunged for Chester, but Chester split into holograms. Flint didn't know which one was the real Chester holding the real remote.

"Flint, we should throw Chester a party," suggested Sam.

Chester and his holograms loved that idea. "It's Chester's time to celebrate!" they cried.

When he heard the word "celebrate," Steve freed himself. He scrambled toward Flint's Celebrationator and pressed the button. The real Chester got covered in glitter. Steve pounced on him and the remote went flying. Flint grabbed the remote and moved his friends to safety.

But Chester wasn't ready to give up yet. He started running away with the FLDSMDFR . . . only to run into Barry and the rest of the living food. When he turned to run the other way, he was blocked by Flint and his friends.

Even Barb had had enough of Chester. She snatched the FLDSMDFR out of his arms. Chester slipped and landed in his food bar machine, but popped back out and thought he was safe when the cheespider caught him!

"It's over!" cheered Sam.

But Flint still had one more thing to do.

Flint returned the FLDSMDFR to the Big Rock Candy Mountain and unplugged Chester's stop button. The FLDSMDFR started up again.

"Be well, old friend," said Flint.

Everyone cheered for the FLDSMDFR and Flint Lockwood! He saved the world . . . again!